AN ENDLESS FRIENDSHIP

A Collection of Stories

By

Sherif Meleka

ISBN: 9798289920249

Imprint: Independently published

When the poet dies—
when the whisper of roses stills,
when the sun's warmth ends,
when his song
sinks into silence...

> When the laughter fades
> from his eyes,
> when wonder vanishes
> from the curve of his brow,
> when cobwebs
> weave across his lips—
> the lips of a seer—
>> That day,
>> the moon will weep.
> That day,
> those long asleep
> will wake
> at the cry of a stone—
> a mute stone
> screaming in every ear.

Sherif Meleka
(When the Poet Dies—2019)

Dedication

To the spirit of my friend, brother and soul-mate, Magdi.
— *Sherif Meleka*

In Memoriam: Magdi Fahmi

In November 2024, I lost my soul mate, my dearest friend Magdi Fahmi, or Dr. Magdi as he usually introduced himself to strangers, despite having spent little or no time practicing medicine. It is impossible to distill the essence of our relationship into a few words. It began in childhood, during our years in primary school, and continued to deepen through middle and high school, into college, medical school, and through the early days of internship and residency. Then I left for America—but we never lost touch. Over the years, our bond only grew.

We used to speak on the phone a couple of times each week, often for hours at a time. Once, he visited me in the U.S., in the 1990's when we traveled together across various cities and states. As he'd always been fond of cars and driving, I let him borrow my sports car then to run around aimlessly a couple of times. On my frequent trips to Egypt, Magdi was always the first to greet me at the airport, and the last to see me off. During my visits, we were—except when sleeping—inseparable, as always.

Together, we crisscrossed Egypt from north to south, from coast to coast. Even when my work took me to distant corners of the country, he would accompany me. Once, we even traveled to Tunisia together for the sake of it. His extended family became mine, and mine became his. My relatives would visit him in Cairo even when I wasn't there—and, over time, they became his close friends.

Our conversations had no boundaries. We knew more about each other than our respective spouses ever did. Sometimes we would sit for hours in his car parked in front of my apartment building, finishing a story one of us had begun as he was dropping me off.

Magdi Fahmi possessed the heart and mind of a poet. He was a man of few words, and when he did speak, it was in a terse, uniquely personal language all his own— his thoughts shared with no one. His constant refrain to me was: *"Observe what people always do—then do the opposite."*

The last years of his life were especially difficult. Once a carefree soul, immersed in the pleasures of living, Magdi was slowly transformed under the weight of illness and the strains of business. I found myself flying back frequently to be close to him during those dark times.

Fortunately, I was with him during his final days, sharing in his pain and suffering for hours each day. Every morning, I would ask him whether he had slept well the night before. And his constant reply was, "No—I only managed a few minutes each hour, and in those, I dreamed of my own funeral."

When I began to write, some 25 years ago, he was the first to support me. He helped me publish my first collection of poems, then my first book of short stories, and later, my first novel. It is for this reason that I've chosen to gather here a collection of stories I wrote with him in mind—some with him as the central figure, others in which he appears among the cast of characters. Naturally, this is a work of fiction, and none of the stories occurred as described within these pages.

— *Sherif Meleka*

The Eyes of Amira

The story had begun many years ago. So deeply buried was it within the folds of time that all traces of the place where it started had faded. In fact, when I recently passed by, I began to doubt whether the entire tale was nothing more than a figment of my imagination. How could I possibly believe that the bond between me and *Amira El-Shawwaf* had started here—when I had confirmed, during my last visit to Cairo, that the red granite-clad train station, which once stood proudly, defying the ravages of time, had vanished entirely? It had once stood right here, in the middle of Mohamed Mahmoud Street in Bab El-Louq. Now, it was gone without a trace, replaced by a new road stretching from Falaki Square—where, on that day long ago, I had begun my walk—intersecting with Sheikh Rihan Street, where my old school stood. I had paused before its colossal gates, and in that moment, I seemed to hear, echoing through the layers of time, the voice of that kindhearted, heavyset man in his tattered clothes. He had stood right here in those distant days, carrying a wooden box before his chest, opening its lid and bowing slightly before us, the young schoolchildren. Inside were small, colored cardboard boxes, each holding a piece of delicious candy and a folded slip of paper bearing one's fortune. In a sweet voice, speaking a French that had always astonished me for its fluency—so at odds with his simple appearance—he would call out:

"Voilà la chance."

I remember the day our story began as if it were yesterday—a radiant winter's day. I was returning from university and had hopped off the bus at Tahrir Square, as was my habit, leaping lightly onto the pavement. The unparalleled cacophony of Cairo swallowed me at once: the deafening roar of traffic, the black plumes of exhaust curling from the buses that still heaved through the square, their passengers crammed so tightly they bulged from both the front and rear entrances, clinging to the metal bars—one foot on the step, one hand gripping whatever they could, while the other hand and foot waved freely, greeting passersby or simply swaying in the wind, if the congestion allowed the vehicle enough speed to stir it.

I darted through the relentless tide of cars, reaching the tree-lined sidewalk beside the American University in Cairo. From there, I slipped past the Lycée Français, where the noise of the square softened somewhat. To my left, a row of cars stood bumper to bumper, forming an impenetrable barrier between me and the frenzied street beyond.

Strangely, I was certain I had recorded these events in my notebook long ago. Yet when I searched for those pages, they had vanished without a trace.

I recall ascending the granite steps into the metro station, crossing the vast hall, and stepping onto the platform. Two trains stood idling on either side. One was about to depart, already bursting with passengers. I chose the second train—there was no need to hurry. I found a seat by the window; many seats were still empty. Across the tracks, the other train remained packed to the brim, its passengers gazing expectantly out of their windows, waiting for departure.

On the platform between the two trains, vendors displayed their wares—freshly baked pastries, homemade sweets, trays stacked with cups of tea and juice. There was a spread of newspapers and magazines, a wooden crate filled with locally made cigarette packs. They treated the metro station as if it were a true railway hub, though in reality, it was nothing of the sort. There was no locomotive pulling its carriages; the trains ran on electricity, powered by overhead wires stretching from Bab El-Louq to Helwan. The longest journey on this line took just over an hour.

I watched the crowd spilling in from the station's grand entrance. Some rushed forward, forcing their way into the already crammed train opposite. Others—like me—ambled toward my train with deliberate ease.

And then, among the throng, I saw her.

Or rather, I saw her eyes first—glimmering amidst a sea of faces.

I knew her at once, even before the rest of her features emerged clearly.

Amira El-Shawwaf—the girl with the most beautiful eyes in our entire college class. Yes, it was her. She walked between my two friends, *Adel Iskandar* and *Shehab Mahmoud*, accompanied by another young man and woman from the university, whom I did not know. As they drew closer, they spotted me. I leaned out the window, waving eagerly. Adel noticed me first and raised his hand in greeting. To my delight, they turned toward my train. In moments, Amira was seated directly across from me, with the other girl beside her, while Shehab took the seat at my side.

To me, Amira had always been a dream—a distant star whose light I could admire from afar but never imagine touching. And yet, here she was, seated across from me. Her luminous eyes met mine at arm's length—so close that, had I reached out, my fingers might have brushed the silken strand of hair that had fallen across her forehead.

I had once asked Adel to introduce me to her, and he had readily agreed. But I had always evaded the moment, much to his amusement. He would mock my unnecessary hesitation, unable to understand my reluctance.

And yet, on this particular day, I do not know from where I summoned the courage.

And yet, there she sat right before me, her small, neatly aligned teeth peeking out between her lips as she smiled. I fought the impulse to turn away, overwhelmed by a sudden tide of shyness. Her hazel eyes, framed by thick, meticulously arranged lashes, were right there in front of me, and so I swilled in their beauty while I could, uncertain when—or if—such a moment might come again.

My heart pounded as Amira El-Shawwaf addressed me directly, asking why we so rarely met on the metro, given that we lived in the same neighborhood and attended the same university every day. She had called me by name. She knew who I was! My words stumbled over themselves in reply, coming out meaningless and fragmented. Just then, salvation arrived in the form of Shehab's voice from beside me, diverting the conversation. I have no recollection of what he said, only that his words flowed with an enviable ease, and that soon, I sensed danger in the way his remarks took on a veiled flirtation. I nudged him sharply in the side to make him stop, but he carried on, unfazed. I was baffled by his persistence, knowing full well about his relationship with another girl at the university—a girl so infatuated with him that she had already spoken to her wealthy family about him and insisted on being with him despite their objections. Their engagement was expected at any moment. So why, then, was he flirting so openly with Amira? And with no regard for my feelings, though he must have known of my admiration for her?

Fury surged through me. I shot him a glance, and he had the audacity to smirk—at first—before finally relenting. I exhaled in relief, though I soon found myself scrambling for something to fill the silence Shehab had left behind. I cast my gaze around, searching for a conversation to grasp onto.

On the platform, I noticed a flurry of movement. I pointed it out to the others, and we watched in curiosity, grateful for the distraction. The opposite train had yet to depart, and instead of boarding ours, passengers were disembarking and loitering on the platform. Perhaps there was a malfunction? We exchanged questioning glances. A shadow of unease flickered in Amira's eyes—only serving to make her more beautiful, as uncertainty lent her features a sudden depth, a maturity that transformed her into a woman exuding raw femininity.

Then, an old man in a faded yellow uniform strode down the platform, calling out in a hoarse, utterly indifferent voice, as if the matter had no bearing on him whatsoever:

"The train's not running. Power's out. The train's not running. Power's out. And it won't be back until late afternoon. If it comes back at all."

We looked at one another, at a loss. Adel broke the silence, asking if we had enough money for a taxi. We laughed awkwardly, as though it were some kind of joke. Then, after a brief pause, he suggested the only viable solution: walking to Maadi.

I considered the distance—ten kilometers, if not more, from Bab El-Louq to Maadi. A three- or four-hour trek. But to me, it felt like a gift from the heavens—an entire afternoon in Amira's company, our first chance to truly talk. And as if contagious, the delight I felt spread among us, transforming our predicament into an impromptu adventure, the kind fate rarely grants. In all our years of taking the metro, never had a power outage forced us to abandon it like this.

And sometimes, a coincidence is worth a thousand plans.

As we crossed Tahrir Square, heading down Sheikh Rehan Street towards the Corniche, the weight laden upon my tongue was lifted. I could not stop talking, and she could not stop responding, peppering me with questions to learn more about me. By the time we reached Maadi, I knew everything about her—the modest circumstances of her family, her sister's marriage to her boss and their subsequent move to the Gulf, where they amassed enough to buy an apartment in Nasr City.

Strangely enough, Shehab had chosen to leave us alone, falling back to walk with Adel and the others, entertaining Amira's friend along the way. No one interrupted our conversation.

I admired her honesty—how she spoke without embellishment or pretense. She told me she had been watching me for some time and had even asked Shehab about me. But, laughing, she mimicked his clipped response: "Forget about him. He's Christian."

I was taken aback. We were university students—not one of us, not even Shehab himself, was thinking of anything serious. We sought nothing more than simple companionship, innocent friendship. So why had he brought religion into it?

I said as much to her, and to my surprise, she told me she had replied to Shehab in the exact same way. We both laughed.

For all her boldness, I soon noticed a hidden shyness beneath it. I saw it in the way her cheeks flushed when my gaze lingered too long upon her hazel depths. She would lower her head, avoiding my eyes, and I would tease her, threatening to expose her secret blush to our friends. She only laughed.

Our meetings multiplied, our mutual admiration deepening. Until, one day, we conspired to escape a dull lecture and sneak off to the cinema. I still remember my astonishment in that darkened theater when I felt her head lean against my shoulder.

I turned towards her as though spellbound, her scent enveloping me. Sensing my movement, she raised her face, her eyes gleaming under the flickering projection light. The darkness wrapped around us, shielding us from the world. I cupped her face gently, lifting it towards me, and pressed my lips to hers—then to her cheek, then to her closed eyelid. On my tongue, the sweetness of strawberries mingled with the brine of the sea.

One of my friends had a father who worked in trade, and owned a car that he always parked in front of their home in downtown Cairo. My friend, in an act of quiet rebellion, had secretly made himself a copy of the key and developed a nightly ritual: once his father had retired for the evening, he would slip out, take the car, and roam the city streets, weaving between downtown and Maadi, where we all lived. He would swing by our homes, gathering us one by one, and we would spend enchanting evenings together, lost in the magic of youth. At the end of the night, he would discreetly refill the tank with a few liters of fuel and park the car exactly as his father had left it, ensuring that nothing seemed amiss.

One evening, emboldened by the thrill of it all, I dared to ask if he would lend me the car—for just one night—so I could take Amira on an evening drive. To my astonishment, he agreed without hesitation. The plan was simple: we would meet at Shihab Mahmoud's house, our usual gathering spot, and from there, I would borrow the car for my rendezvous. I promised to return before ten, giving him enough time to replace the car in its designated spot before his father noticed anything amiss.

Behind the Giza Plateau, under the watchful spirits of the pharaohs, we joined the ranks of countless lovers who, night after night, sought stolen moments of passion in the quiet seclusion of their parked cars—or, in our case, a friend's borrowed one. But tension clung to us, the fear of desert bandits lurking in the shadows, the unspoken agreement that we would go no further than kisses and embraces. I feared failing to protect her, from outsiders, from ourselves. The anxiety dulled the magic of the night. With heavy hearts, we abandoned our ill-fated adventure and returned to the plateau, where we sat upon the hood of the car, nibbling at pastries I had bought in advance, sharing our disappointment in silence.

The drive back to Maadi was a funeral march of unspoken words. But as we neared her home, Amira reached out, placing her hand over my clenched fist on the steering wheel. I turned to her, first with a smile, then with laughter—laughter that seized us both, wild and unstoppable, until she stepped out at the corner near her house, disappearing into the darkness.

I placed the key into my friend's palm, offering him a faint smile of gratitude. He downed the last of his drink in a single gulp, then hurried off to return the car before its absence could be noticed. I was about to leave as well when Shihab stopped me, inviting me for a drink. I hesitated, then agreed.

As we sat together, he asked what had happened. Weariness and tension weighed heavily on me, and for once, I surrendered my pride. I recounted everything—every misstep, every faltering moment—laying bare the story of my failure, or rather, our failure.

But something changed after that night.

She was no longer Amira. Her eyes had lost their light. They were still beautiful, still hazel, but empty.

She no longer sought me out. Every attempt I made to ask what was wrong was met with silence.

Then, one day, she requested to speak with me alone.

She sat across from me, her eyes brimming with unshed tears, spilling over despite her efforts to hold them back. I reached out, trembling, only for her to recoil as though burned. Summoning her courage, she sat upright and told me that Shehab had called for her the day after our night together. He had berated her, shaming her for allowing herself to be with someone like me—a Christian. He had hinted at the consequences, at what he might say if she continued.

The years passed, and our relationship settled into a simple friendship, its deeper memory left untouched. Shehab eventually apologized, saying he had only meant to tease, that things had spun beyond his control. He even apologized to Amira in front of me.

Time, as always, cast its dust upon our story.

And yet, I still search for that vanished train station. I still search for Amira El-Shawwaf, if only to know whether our story truly ended—or if, somewhere, it lingers still.

Good Day to You

I do not know why I awoke this morning enveloped in such joy—overwhelming, explosive joy, suffusing every cell of my being. In truth, the past two days were among the worst I've ever endured—certainly among the bleakest of the last five years. And if you'll allow me, I'd like to explain why. I need to unburden myself to someone.

I was driving home from a vacation that had all but broken my back financially. My wife spoke nonstop throughout the journey, complaining about my passivity and silence in front of her brother-in-law—how he flaunted his newly purchased villa in an upscale neighborhood, how he lamented the sad state of my battered car, dented on all sides from repeated scrapes in the city's congested streets. He had even given me the mocking nickname "the Sphinx," on account of my habitual silence, which his wife—my sister-in-law—found endlessly amusing. She laughed at me constantly.

As usual, I drifted into my own thoughts and responded to none of it. Then, suddenly, I felt the steering wheel become almost immovable. I instinctively glanced in the rearview mirror and managed, with great difficulty, to veer the car into the emergency lane on the right side of the highway, as cars around us zipped past like jet engines.

I got out of the car with a calmness that only provoked further irritation. My wife, raising her voice, asked what had happened. "Dear God, help us! What now?" she cried. I opened the hood and found the culprit— the hose supplying oil to the power steering pump had snapped. This meant I would have to drive the rest of the way without the benefit of power steering, wrestling the stiff wheel like a stone until I could reach a mechanic.

I returned to the car and informed her in clipped tones. I was certain she didn't understand a word of it. But the incident had at least achieved one thing: it silenced her barrage of complaints. And maybe—just maybe—that's why I awoke so happy this morning.

But the story of my suffering didn't end there. Rejoining the highway, I came upon a new exit ramp I hadn't seen before. I slowed slightly to read the sign when a speeding car crashed violently into ours from behind. The driver, distracted by his phone, had seen neither me nor the sign. The rear of my car was destroyed.

Astonishingly, the man emerged from his vehicle furious, shouting that the accident was my fault—that I had slowed too suddenly and should pay for his car's repairs. My wife, momentarily finished with scolding me, found a new outlet for her anger and laid into him with full force, yelling that he had rear-ended us and should be ashamed of using his phone while speeding on the highway.

Their argument escalated. I, ever averse to conflict of any sort, remained silent. Eventually, a police car arrived. The officer declared that if the two parties could not reach some amicable resolution, he would have to tow both vehicles to the nearest station and impound them until morning, when an investigation could determine legal fault. Faced with this ultimatum, both parties reluctantly withdrew.

We returned to our car in silence. I reflected—at least I hadn't been forced to pay for that reckless driver's repairs. Perhaps that, too, was a reason for my surprising joy this morning.

Still, the day's misfortunes weren't finished with me. Nearing our city, I, too, became preoccupied with my phone, trying to find the correct exit and avoid driving an additional several miles—no small feat with a steering wheel like granite and a mangled rear end whose turn signals no longer worked.

My wife tapped my arm urgently. She had noticed the car ahead of us slowing. I looked up to see a bridge looming above, with speed cameras mounted underneath. The driver ahead had panicked and braked sharply. Summoning all my strength, I twisted the stone-heavy wheel and narrowly avoided a collision. Perhaps *that* was another reason for my inexplicable happiness when I awoke today.

We reached home at one in the morning. My wife, exhausted, had dozed off in the final stretch of the drive. I roused her gently and helped her into the house so she could finish her sleep—she usually went to bed by nine at the latest. I carried in our bags and the oversized thermos of tea I had emptied during the drive. Just as I placed them down, my phone rang.

I checked the screen—it was my friend. He never called this late, so I answered immediately. He told me his ex-wife had just passed away after a long battle with cancer. What grieved him even more was the message from his son, informing him of her death—and declaring that he —his own father, would not be welcomed to attend the funeral. He had been estranged from his family for a while due to ethical matters, I find useless to discuss at present.

I did my best to comfort him, though I was physically and emotionally spent from the day' events. I stayed on the line until he was calm. Maybe that, too, is why I woke feeling light and strangely blessed this morning.

But as they say, misfortunes never come alone. Just as I was changing into my pajamas, ready to collapse into bed after a day I knew would be followed by another ordeal—visits to the body shop, the mechanic, a week's worth of stress compressed into twenty-four hours—I decided to relieve my bladder, so I wouldn't be awakened in the night. While doing so, I heard the sound of spraying water coming from the kitchen.

Still urinating—impatiently and painfully, thanks to my swollen prostate—I finished as quickly as I could and rushed to investigate. I found that the hose connecting the faucet to the water purifier had split open, sending a geyser of water shooting across the kitchen. The floor was soaked. Water was rising nearly an inch high, about to overflow the lip that separated the kitchen from the living room.

I shut off the main valve at once and spent the next hour bailing water—seven full buckets—out of the kitchen and into the drain. When I was done, soaked and exhausted, I changed clothes again, fell into bed, and passed out like a man under anesthesia.

The next morning, my cousin from another city called and woke me. I thanked him—I would've slept through the day—and told him everything. Without saying a word, he transferred enough money to cover the car repairs. I thanked him deeply.

I went straight to the mechanic, who replaced the power steering pump. Then I headed to the body shop. There, I sat on a wooden bench for six hours in the searing heat, swatting away flies, shielding my face from wind and dust and the occasional biting insect, watching my beloved car come back to life.

I don't think I've spent that much time tending to—even in a hospital, when my brother was ill.

When the repairs were complete, I drove off, pleased with the results. I went to visit my grieving friend and offer my condolences for the death of his wife and his son's callousness. In return, he invited me out to dinner. I was grateful—realizing, only then, that I hadn't eaten a single thing all day. That meal, simple and warm, felt like a small miracle. Especially since I no longer had a penny to my name after the day's forced expenses.

I returned home drained, parked the car, patted her twice on the hood—my old habit—and climbed upstairs to bed. I collapsed into sleep immediately.

And when I awoke, I found myself smiling, unreasonably content. I felt as though God had been speaking to me throughout those two brutal days, whispering:

The car is not important.

Money is not the point.

Life itself can end in a second—

By accident, or cancer, or some trivial absurdity.

And so, I lay there, pondering the strange, radiant happiness that had filled me when I woke up this morning.

At Sea

He spoke, with resignation in his voice:

"You can lead a horse to water," he said, "but you can't force it to drink." Then he fell silent.

We were out at sea, lifted and lowered by the waves, our feet touching the sandy floor one moment, then drifting weightless the next. We had been enjoying that swaying rhythm, that playful rise and fall, basking in the sun and in each other's company—until he uttered that cryptic phrase. Yes, it was a proverb, a saying I'd heard many times before, but what did he mean by it now? And why had he gone quiet? I thought he was preluding to a story with it, but instead he offered nothing more. I didn't want to press him, so I too held my tongue. We floated on, buoyed by the steady breath of the sea.

Perhaps my silence provoked him. After a while, he began to speak again, but in fits and starts, like a pot

34

boiling over, releasing errant jets of steam from under the lid.

"I must admit," he said, "that this bachelor life of mine has begun to trouble me."

He said no more for several minutes. Then added:

"I'm weary of being alone. In fact, I can no longer stomach the chase—pursuing a new woman, no matter how beautiful or enchanting. I'm tired of the rituals: the endless restaurant dinners, the bar hopping, the thrill of discovering someone new. I've grown sick of waking up beside women whose names I can't even recall. Yes, I used to enjoy it all once. But now, those adventures no longer lift me. I'm repelled by them."

Again, he lapsed into silence. A longer one this time.

I thought back to the early days of our friendship. We had been neighbors on a side street branching off the main road. We used to walk to school together, talking about everything and nothing. We came to know more about each other than our own siblings ever would. We competed in memorizing poems, naming obscure world capitals, recalling the dates of ancient battles, solving difficult math problems. Then we grew older, and our attention shifted to the neighborhood girls—before long, to the girls in our respective colleges. By then, we had ended up in separate faculties, but we stayed close.

At one point, we started dating two sisters. He met one first, then invited me and the other to join him on a group outing. That day marked the beginning of an exuberant, mischievous period of our youth. We fell in love, again and again, and spent many nights confiding in each other, hearts wide open. And when our dreams crashed against the jagged rocks of reality, we became each other's refuge, sharing our heartbreak and nursing our wounds.

Then came the woman I knew—instantly—I would marry. From that moment, a slow drifting apart began. We didn't mean to grow distant, but I was steering toward nesting, toward a settled life, while he remained aloft, soaring through wide skies. He came to see stillness as a form of death, and spoke more and more often of choosing life instead.

We were still rising and falling with the waves, letting the sea cradle and release us, when he broke the silence again, cutting through the stream of memory that had been unfurling in my mind.

"Until I met her."

He paused, then continued.

"I didn't tell you about her before because she reminded me of *you*—of how you looked the day you met your wife. And I remembered how I mocked you then, how I made fun of your sudden infatuation. I felt ashamed. Because here I was, snared just like you had been. The hunter caught in his own trap. I didn't like the reversal. And to be honest, after all these years, I wasn't sure the feeling would last. So, I waited before saying anything. I've never been familiar with this kind of emotion—settled, still, certain. And between you and me, after all this time, I'm not even sure I'm capable of it."

He fell quiet once more.

But this time, I didn't let him disappear into silence. I urged him on.

"Don't stop now, please," I said. "Tell me what happened."

Still rising and falling, still rocked by the breathing tide, he went on:

"My desire for her persisted, no matter how hard I tried to fight it. You remember how I used to boast—I wouldn't let any woman possess me. So, I deliberately dated others, even when my heart wasn't in it. But every time, I ended up thinking of *her*. I'd call her, arrange to see her. The harder I tried to pull away, the closer I found myself drawn."

He paused again, then added:

"What troubled me most was learning she was married. No children. She told me she didn't love her husband anymore, and had considered leaving him long before we met. She said she was his second wife—he had divorced the first because she hadn't borne him children. Still, no children came, and she'd begun to suspect that he was the one with the problem, even from the first marriage. But she didn't dare bring it up. He's volatile. Prone to angry words. She feared he might strike her if she ever voiced that suspicion. Surely, it must have occurred to him too."

He shook his head, frowning at himself.

"And so, I began to reproach myself. How had I allowed myself to become entangled in something so thorny? I had always prided myself on swimming in the sea of my own choosing. Thus, what was I doing now— trapped inside a fish tank? No matter how luxurious or gleaming, it was still a tank. Was I really going to spend the rest of my life circling the same fake coral, brushing past the same plastic weeds? Even if our food floated down to us without effort?"

He dunked his head underwater, then surfaced, speaking more slowly:

"Yet the more I tried to leave, the more I yearned for her."

He looked at me—pleading, searching—as if asking me to toss him a rope and pull him from the depths.

"I finally confessed to her. Told her how conflicted I felt. And to my surprise, she said she felt the same. She had been avoiding me not because she didn't care, but because she couldn't bear the idea of cheating—even on a man she no longer loved. She feared what he might do if she asked for a divorce. So, like me, she chose to withdraw."

He fell silent again. A long silence. Then:

"And yet I—without thinking, I started defending her. I said she had every right to leave him. I even told her that if he tried to stand in her way, I'd confront him myself." He laughed bitterly. "Can you believe I said that? That I volunteered for such a role? I, who've always avoided commitment like the plague. But there I was, not just crossing the bridge—I was sprinting across it. I told myself I was finally facing the unknown, the very thing I'd feared. Maybe *this* was manhood. Maybe *this* was courage."

He let out a deep sigh. He then went on.

"She said she loved me. *Loved* me. And that she'd begin divorce proceedings at once. If he raised a hand, she'd call the police."

He sighed again.

"That was all last week. But now I find I can't move forward. I've tried. Truly. But I wasn't made for that kind of life. And yet—I'm terrified to tell her. How could I now, after she's already asked for a divorce?"

And then he said, as the waves lifted him and let him fall:

"What do I do, my friend? I brought the horse to the water—but I can't make it drink."

And as I rose with a passing wave, then dropped behind it, I found myself admitting: I have no right to offer advice. I, too, have been wrestling lately with quiet questions—about what it means to spend one's entire life with the same woman, day after day, year after year.

Friendship

He struggled to find a parking spot near the house and had to walk nearly a hundred meters to reach it. *"The last time I came here, this street was completely empty... but that was a lifetime ago."* He ascended the stairs slowly, lifting the hem of his black cassock so it wouldn't brush the dusty steps. His mind was wholly occupied by the meeting—no, the confrontation—that he had awaited, for nearly a decade.

In their early youth, they had been inseparable, like twins. Back then, they courted two cousins, lavishing years of affection on them—even into their first years after university. But, as most first loves do, their stories ended in parting. His friend had moved on, while he remained haunted by the love he bore for the cousin. He didn't deny he had loved his friend; he had. But their endless debates had worn him out, and he'd felt a strange relief when time finally placed distance between them. Even those two girls—his own had been the more charming, the more spirited.

Their rivalry had never been spoken aloud, but like so much in life, it shook them in silence. His friend always seemed to win—perhaps through better choices, perhaps through some relentless stroke of fate, or perhaps because of his own poor judgment. He couldn't be sure. But in time, he grew weary of waiting for the outcome of each new contest between them, because he always knew how it would end.

Then came the phone call—from a mutual friend—announcing his return. He had wanted to decline the invitation, but he couldn't bring himself to concede, yet another loss, not one by withdrawal. And so, he came.

Climbing the stairs, he thought: *"But this time, I am in a better place—without a doubt. I'm a priest now! People gather around me daily to hear my counsel. They humble themselves before me, most even kissing my hand. Men and women from every station come running to me, obeying my judgments without question or doubt. Could he ever hope to match that, to rival it in any way? Never. No matter how much success he claims, he cannot best me this time. And even if he flaunts his wealth, I'll remind him: 'The love of money is the root of all evil,' and 'No man can serve two masters: both God and Mammon.' If he boasts of his knowledge, his fame—which has indeed grown recently—I'll bring him back to King Solomon, who in the end declared, 'Our life is but a vapor that appears for a little while, then vanishes away.'"*

"Yes," he thought, *"I will speak of eternal life. That's where I have the upper hand. It's a mystery to the masses, but one I can lead him through. What are a few fleeting decades compared to the treasure of eternity? And he has not seen me since I donned this solemn black robe, this beard streaked with the wisdom of white. I carry the cross wherever I go. He will not be able to withstand the authority of Christ's cross... Even my attire alone will tip the scales. Still, this is just a game among old friends."*

A confident smile played across his face.

He reached the third floor. Letting go of his cassock's hem, he adjusted his head cap and caught his breath. He'd gained weight since being ordained—he now wheezed with the smallest effort. Sometimes he felt ashamed in front of his frail, impoverished parishioners, their bones protruding through their threadbare clothes. How could he preach the virtues of asceticism while carrying this excess flesh?

He shook his head, banishing such negative thoughts, and prepared himself for the long-anticipated reunion.

"How should I greet him?" he wondered. "Should I say 'Welcome back, thank God for your safety,' like any old friend? Or 'Peace and grace be upon you,' as befits a man of the cloth? Should I embrace him? Or step forward holding the cross for him to kiss? Do I meet him as a friend who became a priest, or a priest who used to be a friend? And what if he calls me by my given name? Should I correct him immediately, or let it pass?"

He stood before the door, hesitating for several minutes. Once, he nearly turned back altogether. He chastised himself for all the dark thoughts crowding his heart—how could that befit a man who had renounced the world for the equanimity of true faith?

At last, conscience prevailed. He pressed the doorbell.

His friend opened the door with a wide smile. "Welcome, Abouna!" he cried, embracing him warmly.

He ushered him onto the balcony, where he and another friend had been drinking beer and chatting. The priest followed quietly.

"He brings me into his arena," he thought. *"Thinks that will give him the upper hand. But he's mistaken. This will be my opportunity—my gateway into the glittering vanities of the world he must renounce if he truly seeks eternal life."*

He nodded courteously to the third friend, who rose slightly in his seat and respectfully set aside his glass.

"What will you drink, Abouna?" his host asked.

"Just some cold water, please," he replied.

"Oh, come now," his friend insisted. "At least a soda? I know Catholic priests drink beer and wine—within reason, of course."

The priest interrupted with a gentle smile: "A soda will do just fine. Though truly, a cold glass of water is more than enough."

His host disappeared and returned shortly with both.

They exchanged polite questions. The friend asked about his wife and children— "They've married now, and I'm a grandfather." He returned the question, only to remember too late that the priest had once been married to a woman who left him, unable to bear life with him.

The priest answered coolly: "Our eldest daughter married recently. I have a son from my new wife—he's a year and a few months old."

His friend laughed. "The same age as my youngest grandson!"

"The scoundrel," the priest thought. *"Another jab. But it's just a skirmish. The war is what matters."*

His friend, still smiling, asked casually, "Was it difficult to get remarried, after all that?"

With composure, the priest explained that since his first marriage had been under the Catholic rite and he had since converted to Orthodoxy, it was declared void, and his new marriage was legitimate under the new rite. Then, shifting the conversation, he said with a laugh, "But I came to hear about you, our beloved star!"

The friend leaned back slightly. "A star? Hardly! I'm happy, that's all. I've done more than I ever dreamed. If I died today, I'd go in peace."

The priest's eyes gleamed. *"He's walked right into it,"* he thought. *"And I didn't even push him."*

With feigned innocence, he asked, "And if you did die today—God forbid—are you certain of what comes next?"

His friend chuckled. "Is anyone? I mean, truly certain?"

The priest raised his glass and replied solemnly, "Yes—if you have faith."

"But faith," his friend said gently, "is believing in what we cannot see. Certainty, though, is knowing what is true. And in matters beyond life, we don't have facts— we have sacred texts we believe in. They inspire faith, but they are not empirical truths."

The priest's voice sharpened: "Do you not believe in the truth of the Bible?"

His friend sipped his beer. "I do believe. But most of what's in it lacks scientific foundation—from Adam and Eve, to the Flood, to Moses and Pharaoh, to Jonah and the whale. I see those stories as symbolic—meant to convey deeper truths, to show us the divine relationship with humankind. Scripture isn't a science book, nor a history text. These stories aren't there just to be believed, but to be understood and learned from. But in any case, these are just my beliefs—I don't claim they are the truth."

The priest smiled with pity and asked softly, "Then you don't believe in life after death?"

"I never said that," his friend replied quickly. "I do believe in life after death. And I believe that because of God's infinite love, all people will be saved—whether they call it Heaven, or the Kingdom, or Jannah, or Nirvana, it's all the same."

The priest straightened, setting his glass aside, and spoke with the weight of holy authority: "Then what of Christ's own words? 'I am the door—if anyone enters by me, he will be saved.' Why would He say that, if everyone can enter without Him?"

His friend answered calmly, provoking him more: "I believe that. But others—many others—have their own sacred texts guiding them to salvation. God spoke to each according to what they could understand, even before the so-called Abrahamic faiths. Sun-worshipers, moon-worshipers, animal-worshipers—they believed what they did by divine will. God made all people in His image. Do you think a father with seven children—like the seven billion alive today—would condemn four of them to eternal damnation just because they were born into a different faith?"

The priest let out a nervous laugh. "You intellectuals! Always dodging! But I... I follow the Bible. I don't pretend to be deep like you. I don't know the fate of non-Christians. But I know what Scripture says: Christ is the only way. If you don't believe that, you'll have no share with Him."

His friend smiled. He thought, nevertheless; *"He believes he owns the truth. That he alone knows the mind of God. I won't stoop to quoting Jesus on divorce, or condemn him for his second marriage. He's still one of God's children."*

He took another sip of his beer and said, "I told you—I believe in Christ, in the Gospel. Doesn't Scripture say, 'God desires all people to be saved and to come to the knowledge of the truth'? That's my faith. I trust in it for myself. And I trust in His love for others as well. Love never fails."

That final line landed like a sword. A direct quote. The priest could neither refute nor dismiss it. So, he turned to the third man—silent until now, nursing his drink and cracking peanuts—and asked sharply, "And you? Do you believe non-Christians will enter the Kingdom?"

The man shrugged. "No, I don't think so."

The priest exhaled in relief. A sacred aura returned to him, and with a puffed chest, he declared, "Please reflect deeply, my friend. The Devil can plant doubts to lead you astray. I only say this out of love, and concern for your soul."

He rose, excused himself for another appointment, and left—vowing never to return, never to speak with that friend again. The man, he thought, was lost to the world and had surely forfeited his soul.

And so, he departed, saddened, despairing the loss of yet another soul.

The Sorcerer

At first glance, he seemed indistinguishable. Aside from a lingering trace of youthful charm—suggesting a past tinged with mischief and adventure—*Fakhry Zehni* struck most people as utterly ordinary. In fact, some of our mutual friends considered him less than ordinary: too quiet, expressionless, always seated in the farthest corner during lively gatherings, absorbed in his phone, or dutifully filming our get-togethers not out of joy, but as if he were tasked with documenting them.

I can't recall ever hearing Fakhry Zehni express an opinion, voice a complaint, or even admit to the sort of anguish or heartache that splits a man's life in two. Nor do I remember seeing him truly joyful nor merely pleased—not once. He never laughed freely, unless we were watching a film. His demeanor was a constant hum of neutrality—except, perhaps, when I asked him directly for his view on something. Then, and only then, he'd respond with startling honesty—whether to admit quiet joy or to unveil some brutal truth. For that reason, I always considered him my truest and dearest friend.

One night, we gathered to bid farewell to Henry, a friend soon to travel. I brought a fine bottle of whiskey as a gift, which he promptly uncorked and shared generously. Our group grew merrier with every glass. Among the guests were my old friend *Tomi* and a mysterious Gulf woman no one else seemed to know. By chance, she ended up seated beside Fakhry. The music deepened the revelry—a young man arrived with an oud and a honeyed voice, singing classics. At some point, one of the women, swept away by the melodies, got up and danced with unselfconscious delight until dawn. We left that night buoyant and wishing our host a safe journey.

A few days later, while driving with Fakhry through Cairo, I happened to voice my discomfort at the sight of a young boy, no older than ten, straining to unbolt, lift and replace a battered car tire at a tire-repair-shop. Fakhry looked over at me, blank as usual, and said nothing.

An hour later, we were passing through our once-proud neighborhood—now weathered, overcrowded, its villas crumbling, its trees choked by dust and traffic. Amid the chaos, a blind young man stepped off the curb ahead of us. His face bore no eye-balls at all, only smooth hollows of skin. Horns blared from every direction.

"Watch out, Fakhry!" I shouted. "You'll hit him!"

With his usual composure, Fakhry swerved neatly and drove on as though nothing had happened.

"Stop the car," I said. "I'll help him cross. He's going to get himself killed trying to manage alone in this maddened traffic chaos."

Fakhry didn't slow down. He merely said, eyes on the road, "That lad *chooses* to cross in the middle of this mess. He's a beggar, no doubt. If he weren't, he'd have someone helping him."

"What if he has no one?" I challenged.

"Then he should stay home."

"For the rest of his life? The man's blind, Fakhry. He has no eyeballs. His vision isn't coming back tomorrow."

He said nothing more—just pressed the accelerator. A moment later, he added:

"You've changed. You were upset by the boy changing tires, and now you want to play savior for some blind man in traffic. This is our daily life. It's not going to change. We're not going to become perfect, just because *you* want us to."

We moved on in silence.

That evening, we were invited to a dinner at a stylish restaurant. It was to celebrate a friend's recent award. By chance, I was seated beside our hostess, Tomi, while Fakhry sat at the far end, next to an older man I didn't recognize. The table buzzed with cheer and congratulations.

Between bites of appetizers, Tomi leaned toward me and asked, "Is your friend a *sorcerer*?"

I laughed, uncertain of what she implied. "What do you mean, *sorcerer*?"

She nodded toward Fakhry. "Look at him—he's *enchanted* my husband!"

I glanced down the table. The two men were deep in quiet conversation, disengaged from the general din.

"That man's your husband?" I asked.

She nodded. "He hasn't spoken a word to anyone else here. Just to your friend, Fakhry Zehni. I've never seen him like this."

She paused, then added: "And a few nights ago, at Henry's apartment, that Gulf woman who came with me? She left my house at two-thirty in the morning to go see *him*. Your friend is a sorcerer, no doubt about it."

Her words lingered with me. Was he really? How else to explain it? That mute, calm man—he had seduced her friend, and now mesmerized her husband, without so much as lifting a finger. And yet, when I asked him to "steal away" the misery of a working child or help a blind man cross the road, he scoffed. If he *were* a sorcerer, couldn't he return sight to the blind man? Or, at the very least, let *me* help him, or slightly sympathize with my objection to a child laborer?

The next day, I decided to test Tomi's theory. Fakhry and I were meeting an old friend of ours—one of the most compassionate men I know. He was nearly blind himself, the result of a degenerative optical illness ten years back.

Over coffee, I recounted the story of the child manual worker and that of the blind man. I expected a strong rebuke of Fakhry's indifference; certain our friend would take my side.

I was already relishing my moral victory; my hands rubbing in triumph beneath the table. Asking our nearly unsighted friend whether a blind man should be helped to cross the street was hardly a fair question. Besides, his refined human compassion would, of course, be expected to side against children being forced into such harsh labor. When our friend began to speak—in his gentle voice—agreeing *completely* with Fakhry's perspective.

The boy, he said, was typical and ordinary for our society. And as for the blind man—he was most likely a professional beggar, or else he'd never cross a chaotic street alone in broad daylight.

It was then I recognized: Fakhry Zehni was a *sorcerer*.

An Endless Friendship

Love in the Pace of Murad Fahim

One evening, the handsome man sat behind his desk. A dull brass nameplate, half-buried beneath a mountain of clutter, bore his name etched in Latin letters: *Murad Fahim*.

The room was modest, its walls bare, nearly swallowed by a single, hulking wooden desk cluttered with papers, books, and the debris of daily routine. Yet it exuded a strange comfort, a quiet warmth, like a room that had learned to breathe with its owner.

The air conditioner growled as it transformed the furnace of Cairo open-air into a breeze that teased the hairs on his head, which stood alert as he hunched over his computer screen. His fingers tapped the keyboard intermittently, pausing only so his right hand could embrace the mouse, guiding it with the precision of a surgeon. A faint smile played at the corners of his lips, betraying a certain pleasure in the work at hand.

By day, he was a radiation oncologist at a modestly known private hospital. By night, he helmed a small software company he owned outright. In both realms—medicine and tech—he chose his clientele with surgical care. He disdained the masses, harboring open contempt for them. He reserved his respect for the cultured elite—those who spoke foreign languages fluently or hailed from wealthy, well-educated families, like himself. He would sooner sacrifice profit and success than stoop below this threshold of association.

He was not born bourgeois, nor had he ever been arrogant. Life, in all its sharp and splintered experiences, had carved him into this shape.

There was one exception to this rule—women. With them, all classes dissolved. He welcomed them in every flavor: educated or not, refined or rustic, young or old. His elitism turned socialist in their presence—a transformation so pure even his most radical leftist friends envied him.

Then, as if to punctuate the silence, the phone rang. He lit a cigarette quickly, then answered:

"Hello?"

A strange voice replied—distant and flickering, like a signal across static. He adjusted the receiver, trying to extract clarity from the distortion. Slowly, the words assembled themselves:

"Mr. Murad, we've missed you... we'd love to see you... would you mind if I visited your office?"

He recognized the voice, though only just.

"Ah... of course. Please, you're most welcome. Not at all. No inconvenience whatsoever."

He set the receiver down and returned to his work. But the words lingered.

He reached for his cigarette, inhaled.

Sheikh Farid Boulos, himself, this time? You won't stop bothering me, will you, Sarah?

They had married twenty years ago, though their true union lasted only two. During that brief era, she bore their second daughter, and the marriage unraveled.

She was devout—her world walled off from his entirely. Her life revolved around worship and service: feeding the poor, aiding children, visiting the disabled, even befriending the city's garbage collectors. She tended her aging parents, mingled with her two virtuous brothers—both pious businessmen—and their equally saintly wives. She longed for him to complete the circle.

64

If he, too, could become "good," joy would rain down on them all.

But he loved life in its unruly hues: late nights with friends, cold beer in smoky bars. More than that, he loathed her way of life. In time, he came to loathe her—and with her, the entire haloed orbit of her family.

Outwardly, they shone. They were Egypt's crème de la crème—the phrase itself borrowed, with insufferable pride, from French. But he knew the truth: a pageant of hypocrisy, deceit, and malice. They despised others, clawed at each other behind bright smiles, and their family gatherings were bloodless arenas of envy and theft. They bragged about it. One would boast of stealing a deal from his own brother, likening it to plucking meat from a lion's jaws.

Murad was no saint, but at least he didn't pretend. He never hid behind a veil.

He knew his looks had opened doors. He'd never pursued a woman—except his wife, a mistake he regretted for the rest of his life. After her, it was the women who sought him, as one of them once confessed. He didn't initiate—but he was quick to catch the bait.

Still, that call from Sheikh Farid haunted him. What did the man want? Their lives had no overlap.

Surely it wasn't about software—Farid's world lay galaxies away from programming. He was a church elder, a pillar in the congregation Sarah and her family were so proud of. Even in medicine, there was no link: patients never approached him directly. They came via oncologists—like his friend—when a late-stage cancer case met Murad's social and intellectual criteria.

And Sheikh Farid had said he *missed* him, wanted to *see* him, as though they were close. They weren't. Farid was a pioneer of the very brand of false piety that Sarah's circle thrived on. Murad didn't blame him—it was a personal choice. In fact, he held a grudging respect for the man, largely because he spoke fluent English with the occasional Western visitors to the church. But he was no friend.

No. This was Sarah's doing—another attempt to herd him toward the pasture of the pious. He had no claim to righteousness, but he refused their synthetic version of it.

To him, faith was a secret thread between man and God. To them, it was lifestyle: worn on one's face, plate, clothes, front door, and even rear windshield.

What would he do if Farid actually came? The man was old, respected. Murad wouldn't be rude. But he'd surely make it clear he had no time for religious fellowship.

Weren't they the ones who preached freedom of belief?

Empty slogans. The bait was always sweet—until the hook tore your throat.

No. He would not bite. Let Farid come first—then they'd see.

He didn't ask Sarah about the call. Weeks passed. Sheikh Farid never came. The matter drifted out of mind.

Until another evening, as Murad immersed himself in work, the phone rang again.

"Hello?"

A soft, feminine voice this time.

He straightened in his chair, instinctively preparing the old protocols, ready to catch her—should she be willing to leap.

"Dr. Murad? I'm Habiba.[1]"

"Habiba… someone's sweetheart, perhaps?"

---

[1] Habiba in Arabic means lover.

"Haha—no, that's my name. Sheikh Farid Boulos asked me to call you."

The name struck like a slap. His enthusiasm drained instantly.

"Ah… I see. And what can I do for you?"

"He asked me to visit you."

Immediately, his voice shifted back to playful:

"The Sheikh sent you—to visit me? When?"

"Yesterday—no, I mean now. Do you mind if I come by?"

"But… I'm alone, I mean, I'm here by myself."

"So am I. Haha. Are you afraid of me? Haha…"

She laughed—a teasing sound—but kept a certain formality, like a schoolteacher welcoming a timid student on his first day. He ignored the undertone and replied, with a laugh laced with meaning:

"Me? Afraid of *Habiba*? Never."

"Good. I think I'm near your office. Just a few minutes."

The call ended. He leapt from his seat, opened the window to purge the smoke, straightened the room in a frenzy. Then—doorbell.

He opened it and was struck speechless.

She was the ugliest woman he had ever seen.

Narrow eyes, an enormous nose, a mouth wide enough to swallow his head, crooked teeth, and hair ironed flat, streaked clumsily with yellow strands. He stepped aside in defeat, allowing her in, shoulders slumping in resignation.

What could he do? She was sent by Sheikh Farid— or worse, by Sarah. His hands were tied.

But once she passed the grotesque canvas of her face, the rest of her was... startling.

A large, bouncing bosom. Full hips that swayed like loaded baskets. A tight green dress clung to her thighs, revealing two pale, shapely legs. Taken together—it wasn't a total loss. And anyway, in the dark, beauty and ugliness wear the same mask.

After a brief preamble, the purpose of her visit emerged, and he confirmed what he already suspected: Sarah had orchestrated this.

But Habiba surprised him. She was, in fact, devout. Unmarried by choice, she had devoted her life to God's service. She worked at a preschool, ministered to the poor, traveled to remote places to help those in need. She collected donations, solved crises, and even housed the homeless in her own apartment when she had to.

His original plan crumbled.

He slumped, lit a cigarette, exhaled a long cloud of smoke.

"But why come here?" he asked.

She told him, with guileless sincerity, that both Sheikh Farid and Sarah had sent her. She had come to beg him to treat a poor man brought to the capital after his condition had worsened.

Her crooked teeth became more pronounced as she smiled, yet her joy didn't falter. She looked at him with those narrow eyes, not once lowering her gaze. Still, her hands danced expressively as she spoke.

Her body's strange allure nearly eclipsed the horror of her face.

He replied, grudgingly:

"Treat him? Hmm... why not take him to a public hospital?"

"We did. They said he must wait his turn. Do you know when that might be?"

He drifted further from his scheme. Even after conceding that her body might compensate for her face, he now saw it was futile.

"And what do you want from me?" he asked.

Then a wicked idea sparked.

"Do you have the oncologist's referral?"

She laughed.

"Of course, doctor. You think I'd forget that?"

She reached into her bag and pulled out a yellow envelope.

He was caught. He leafed through the papers, reading them closely. He was, after all, a meticulous physician.

He returned them with finality.

"Fine. Bring him to the hospital tomorrow. Noon."

"But I'm at the preschool until two..."

He cut her off, irritated.

"Then bring him at three-thirty. Not a minute later. The session will take at least two hours."

The next day, she arrived early, supporting a tall, frail man with sallow skin and sunken cheeks. He leaned heavily on her, his arm over her shoulder, her generous chest pressed against his bony ribcage. Murad noted the contact—but the man groaned in pain, oblivious to everything else.

Murad instructed the nurse. Within moments, the man was prepped, a needle in his arm, fluids entering his body.

Murad sat. Habiba sat across from him.

He told her he'd charge no fee—but she would need to cover the equipment costs.

She nodded gratefully.

Time passed in silence. Murad studied her ruined face, trying to ignore the light rising from her spirit. She, in turn, looked at him—enchanted by his attractiveness, touched by his mercy, by accepting to treat an unknown person free of charge.

He finally asked:

"Why didn't you ever marry…"

She answered shyly,

"I haven't found him yet."

"But—all of those?"

"I'd rather give myself in service to them all, even though each one wants to be served as if he were the only one."

The treatment continued for weeks. She brought the man back three times a week, always at three-thirty sharp. Each morning, Habiba sent Murad a short greeting and a bouquet of flowers electronically. Strangely, he began replying, message for message.

One day, she asked him,

"Why do you live like this?"

"What do you mean?"

"You deliberately bury your angelic nature in the arms of the devil."

"Speak to me in words I can understand. No angels. No devils."

"But you do understand what I mean."

"How can I understand when you speak of things unseen?"

"Don't you believe in God?"

"I believe in the human being—who cannot deceive God, no matter how he tries."

She recognized the futility of her attempt and fell silent. She knew with certainty: his essence was pure—a rare pearl cast in mud. It was hers to recover, to cleanse with care, until it shone again. His generous attention to *Saber*, given without demand or reward, astonished her.

With time, he began to seep into her heart, a heart green and untouched, never grazed by Cupid's arrow. He was handsome and successful in his work, always warm and courteous in speech—and most remarkably, he respected her. He had never tried to draw close or pull her toward him, as every other man had done.

She asked him,

"Do you love your wife?"

"Of course not. But how many men have told you otherwise?"

Habiba laughed. But all the others had used their lack of love for their wives as a gateway to something with her—except him.

"And you—have you ever loved before, Dr. Murad Fahim?"

"Once. When I was a medical student. She was a classmate."

"Was?"

"Yes—was. She was a pure vitality, full of laughter and brilliance. And then—gone. She dove into the sea and never came out. After that, I couldn't love again."

"Were you engaged? I mean, before she died?"

"No. Never. I didn't even tell her I loved her."

"So how long did this Platonic affair last?"

"A few months... maybe. I can't remember."

"Do you—excuse my asking—but do you still have a picture of her?"

"No. There was one photo of us with a group of friends, but it vanished. I don't know when or how. I searched everywhere once—but it was gone."

"Then how can you be sure you loved her? Maybe she's just your excuse. A way to assure yourself you've loved once—so you never have to face the possibility that you've never truly fallen in love."

The man's treatment ended. Saber returned to his village. Habiba had no more reason to see Murad Fahim.

Two long days passed. Seeing him had become all she could think of. She continued to send her morning messages. His replies grew terser, sometimes tinged with mockery.

On the third morning, she wrote:

"I'm in the middle of a crisis that's tearing me apart. I have to see you."

"What happened?"

His curt tone, the indifference in that single line, ignited her fury. She didn't reply.

The next morning, noticing her silence, he messaged her first:

"I haven't heard from you. Are you alright? I can see you in my office this afternoon."

In the four days since she'd last seen him, her energy had drained away. She entered his office faint and faltering, collapsing into the first chair she found. He reached out to steady her before she missed it and hit the floor. Instincts sharpened, like a doctor's would in the emergency ward. He examined her face, under her eyes, the color of her lips, her nails. Then his fingers found her wrist, searching for her pulse. Glancing at his watch, he muttered,

"What happened?"

She snatched her hand from his grip.

"I'm not ill. I don't need a doctor."

"Your pulse is racing. You're pale and weak. You've lost so much weight in just a few days."

"As I told you—I'm in the middle of a crisis!"

"What crisis?"

"I realized... I love you."

"And that's the crisis?"

"A war is tearing me up inside. How do I fall in love with a married man?"

"First, you didn't decide to fall in love. Or you would've already had—more than once with any other man you've known. Second, a man who neither loves nor lives with his wife isn't truly a husband. Third—"

She cut him off.

"Enough! If even half of what you say were true, I wouldn't feel what you see written across my face right now!"

"I'm not responsible for your hidden desire to torture yourself."

"Don't you see how my life of service and devotion clashes with loving a married man?"

"And am I responsible for your contradictions, too? In any case, I'm more concerned about your heart rate and your condition. Do you want me to examine you now, or would you prefer I take you to another doctor?"

"It's nothing. Physically, I'm fine."

"You don't get to decide that. I'm the doctor. And I'm offering you two choices."

"I know my body. But fine—if it puts your mind at ease, examine me. What do you want me to do?"

"Just lie down on that couch, and unbutton your shirt."

He stepped into the other room and returned with a stethoscope and blood pressure cuff.

"Your pressure's low. Pulse still racing."

He placed the stethoscope against her chest, moving it from place to place. Her clammy skin was damp with sweat. She flinched and pushed his hand away.

"Sorry—I can't bear your touch. I feel dizzy. Forgive me."

"Alright, calm down. I'll make you something warm to drink."

She closed her eyes. She didn't button her shirt. A smile of unearthly peace softened her face. She was adrift in a bliss she'd never known. Meanwhile, Murad was in the kitchen, preparing hot hibiscus tea.

When he returned, the sight of her startled him. He thought she had fainted.

"Habiba? Habiba!"

His voice shook her. She sat up, dazed, and began buttoning her shirt in a flutter of nervous hands. For the first time, Murad saw the fullness of her chest. In that instant, he was no longer Murad the doctor—but the man. He set the tea down with a wicked smile.

"Drink the hibiscus—and leave the buttons to me."

He didn't wait for permission. His fingers played across her chest with hungry delight. Yet—he couldn't bring himself to kiss her, as he would have with any other woman at this moment. Her ugliness sobered him. It triumphed over desire.

She, meanwhile, was lost in ecstasy, a rapture she'd never imagined, her body trembling with wave after wave of spasms she could not control.

Never had he known a woman like this, despite all his affairs over the years.

All this from the touch of my fingers? What if—

But he froze. She might actually faint. Her eyes were still shut, her limbs convulsing silently, her breath short like someone possessed.

When he stopped, it was as if someone had yanked the electric cord from the socket. Her eyes opened. The trembling ceased. She adjusted her hair and clothes, hands shaking, and suddenly burst into tears.

He didn't know what to do. Her face twisted in sorrow, making her even more grotesque. He couldn't bear to look at her. How had he taken her innocence so

80

easily? He knew she had no future with him, yet he hadn't hesitated to lunge when the opportunity came— like any beast pouncing on prey when hunger strikes. And still, all he did was turn his face away and pat her shoulder gently, muttering:

"Drink your hibiscus. You'll feel better. I'm so sorry. I didn't mean to..."

"I'm sorry too, Murad. I shouldn't have come today."

It was the first time she said Murad without the formality of "Doctor." He felt sickened by her plainness, ashamed that he had let her come so close.

She kept crying as she straightened her clothes, crying as she shook his hand goodbye, as she descended the stairs, all the way home.

He felt a certain dull ache for about two hours, which he spent in his office doing nothing but smoking cigarettes, one after another. Then he gathered his things and left. He went to his favorite bar, where he found an old friend. They drank beer together until the whole thing faded from his mind.

Habiba, however, cried for seven days straight. She asked the school principal for a sick leave—her health was truly failing. She spent those days weeping, praying for God's forgiveness, pleading for another chance to redeem herself.

A second chance to save Murad Fahim.

To pull him into the circle of the righteous.

The Survivor

The heat was lethal.

We lay stranded in our car, buried within a nest of vehicles streaming in from every direction into the chaos of *Sayyida Aisha Square*. Traffic had—as always—suffocated, thanks to a bus driver who decided he had every right to cut across the square from the far right to the far left, aiming to pass beneath the overpass. He was going in our direction, yet we hadn't moved in nearly half an hour. The driver of a taxi insisted he had the right of way because he had reached that spot first.

Small cars and hulking buses besieged us from all sides. The AC had long since given up—the engine was far too hot. We opened all four windows, but the temperature in the square must have reached the boiling point. As for the humidity—don't even ask. Car exhaust thickened the air until it became an invisible soup, swirling in shimmering waves above the vehicle roofs. It was as if the world around us had begun to boil.

Suddenly, a chorus of horns erupted from every direction, perfectly synchronized, as if all the drivers had secretly agreed on this moment. It was the declaration of collective fury, the trumpet blast before a battle. I braced myself for war, if fate didn't intervene.

"Move, you infidels!"

The driver of the car beside ours bellowed. He was so close his voice pierced my ear like a cannon blast. I clapped my hand over it and turned to locate the source of the explosion. *This is the spark*, I thought. *This is how it starts.*

He glared at me, daring me to utter even a syllable of protest. I chose the safer path and turned my eyes away. The man had clearly reached the end of his tether and needed only the faintest excuse to pour his fury on me. I was nearest. I was within reach. The others were out of arm's length, safe from his righteous wrath.

My friend at the wheel reached every minute or so for a pink tissue from the box before him, dabbed at his streaming face, and stuffed the sodden paper into a bag hanging from the gearshift. He's not much of a talker in general, but today—whatever this day was—he'd gone completely silent. Even when I asked why he hadn't taken the Corniche route, he said nothing. I fiddled with the radio dial, but it emitted a screeching howl, so I switched it off immediately. I looked to him for some reaction, but he was busy lighting what must have been his fourth or fifth cigarette.

I leaned past him, peering across the square, beneath the overpass, toward the side we were supposedly heading to—if "marking time" counted as direction of motion. I could just make out the row of shops opposite the *City-of-the-Dead*. A low wall surrounded each tomb, a wooden door—usually shut—set in the center of every enclosure. One stood open, letting me glimpse the life within: clotheslines strung with drying laundry, children chasing each other in circles, and a woman crouched before a stove, stirring a pot from which steam rose steadily. An ordinary domestic scene—except it played out among the dead, who slumbered beneath the ground, while the living, in this infernal heat, looked to be dying slowly above it.

Two girls in a little red car, two vehicles ahead, leaned far out their windows, torsos twisting as they shouted in voices half-laughing, half-pleading.

"Come on, people, enough already—we've got families who'll disown us!"

My friend burst out laughing.

At last, some sign that he, too, was alive. I, on the other hand, didn't know what to say. I was suffocating— but I dared not complain, lest I make him feel guilty for choosing this road. But this heat! And not a single breeze. The air, poisoned with exhaust fumes, laced with cigarette smoke. And just a few meters away: the silent tombs of the dead. *Is there no deliverance, Lord?*

Then—music.

It started as a murmur, far off, then grew swiftly louder, veering toward my window—toward me and toward the expiative driver I'd been fearing.

But the tune—it was joyous. Infectiously so. I twisted my torso toward the sound. It filled the square. Heads turned in all directions, trying to locate it. The rhythm pulsed like the clapping of many hands around a winter bonfire, or the synchronized stomping of men cheering on a woman dancing in their midst.

And there he was.

A young man with dark, gleaming skin and a bright smile, balancing a woven reed tray stacked high with loaves of bread on his left hand, while his right gripped the handlebars of an astonishing bicycle. Mounted on either side of the handlebars were two loudspeakers, blaring the music. Between them, nestled in the center, was a cassette player powering the whole affair. And at the outermost ends of the handlebar—two electric fans aimed directly at his face.

His feet worked the pedals steadily, which in turn powered a tiny dynamo: the music, the fans, the miracle. Colorful ribbons fluttered from the ends of the handlebars, the spokes of the wheels, and the pedals.

He darted through the paralyzed traffic like a shooting star, joyous, agile, dancing between cars as if they were trees in a forest. Drivers gawked at him, stunned. His appearance—and his vanishing, just moments later—was enough to silence every blaring horn. Then, as suddenly as he came, he was gone.

An Endless Friendship

89

A Bird...

(عصفور...)

A bird...
oppressed,
its strength dissolves.
It longs to flutter—
to soar far away...
But tears mist its eyes,
the burden—too grave.

The perch beneath it
has left deep marks—
wrinkles... scars...
betraying its years.

It kicks with one leg,
its body trembling—
thrashing, resisting,
straining to flee,
stretching, unfurling
its wings—
tied down, pulled taut—
and we heard its cries.

With fierce resolve,
it tears at the cords,
whispers *"Soon now…"*
murmurs *"It's near…"*
"I'm almost flying!"

> On a breeze of silk,
> it dreams to rise,
> its heart blooming
> with each beat.

It cries *"Oh, my!"*
and the hush of the world
fills its ears.

> Then the bird
> spreads its wings—
> and soars again…

> And I hear nothing
> but the throb of my heart.
> Or is it the heartbeat of the cosmos?

Voices… and song…
and no one beside me—
only light…
and joy…
and seas of brilliance.

I glimpsed birds—
eyes shining—
circling the throne...
around my Lord.

And I was filled with light.
And I became light.
And I flew, a wanderer—
without feather,
without wing.

Sherif Meleka (The Bird—2006)

Made in the USA
Columbia, SC
03 July 2025

60072636R00057